Fancy NANCY'S®

Perfectly Pink Playtime Purse

Based on *Fancy Nancy* written by Jane O'Connor

Cover illustration by Robin Preiss Glasser

Interior illustrations by Robin Preiss Glasser

HARPER FESTIVAL

An Imprint of HarperCollinsPublishers

P9-CQH-828

There's Nothing Like a Spa Day

Nancy is having a super-deluxe spa day in her clubhouse. Help transform the clubhouse by drawing and coloring in what is missing. Add some stickers to give the scene some *je ne sais quoi!*

Fancy Fingers

A beautiful manicure makes any outfit elegant. Draw a line from the nail polish bottle to the matching color on Nancy's nails.

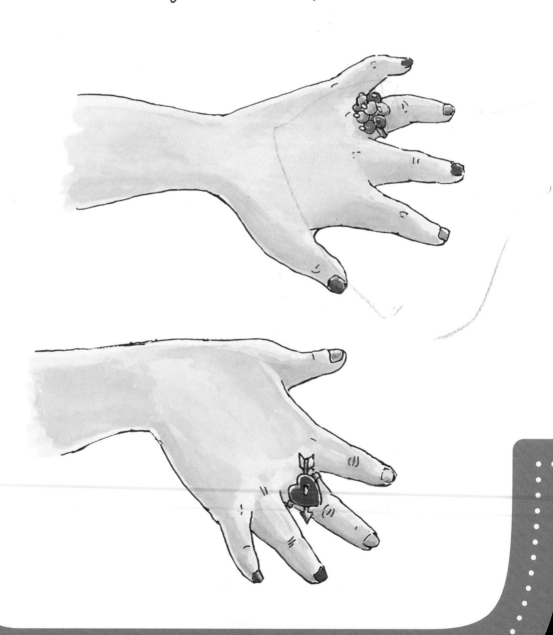

Perfectly Pink

Bonjour Blue

Forever Fuchsia

Golden Glimmer

Strawberry Parfait

Lotus Blossom

Luscious Lime

Sunburst

Cherry Pie

Black Velvet

Spa Mobile

Nancy is making a pretty mobile for her spa day, but she still needs a few things to make it complete. Add more spa-themed things to help Nancy finish the mobile.

Tea Time

Find the stickers to finish the picture.

Makeover Time!

Help Nancy apply some makeup to her mom's face to transform her from beautiful to exquisite.

Poet Tree

The Poet Tree is almost ready for family day, when Nancy and her friends will read their poems. But it still needs more leaves and flowers! Help finish the tree by drawing in colorful leaves and flowers.

Leaf It to Nancy

Nancy loves collecting the most beautiful fall leaves she can find. Color in the leaves to complete her collection.

Nancy's Doodles

This is a collection of doodles that Nancy drew.
Help fill in the missing items by coloring them in.

Glamorous Gifts

Ooh, glamorous gifts! Color these presents and draw your favorite decorations.

Time for Tea!

Make this tea pot fancier by coloring it in and adding stickers.

RSVP

Nancy has prepared an elegant tea party for Marabelle and her friends. But where are all the guests? Find them and put them on the page.

Bonjour, Bree!

Draw lots of flowers on Bree's dress, using your favorite colors.

Pirate Paraphernalia!

Nancy's sister is completely obsessed with pirates.
Circle the items on the shelf that are pirate-themed.

A Fancy Topper

Draw three more glamorous hats to go on Nancy's coatrack.

At the Playground

Find the stickers to finish the picture.

Walk the Runway

Nancy is putting on a fashion show. Connect the items on the floor and stairs by drawing ribbon between them to complete the runway.

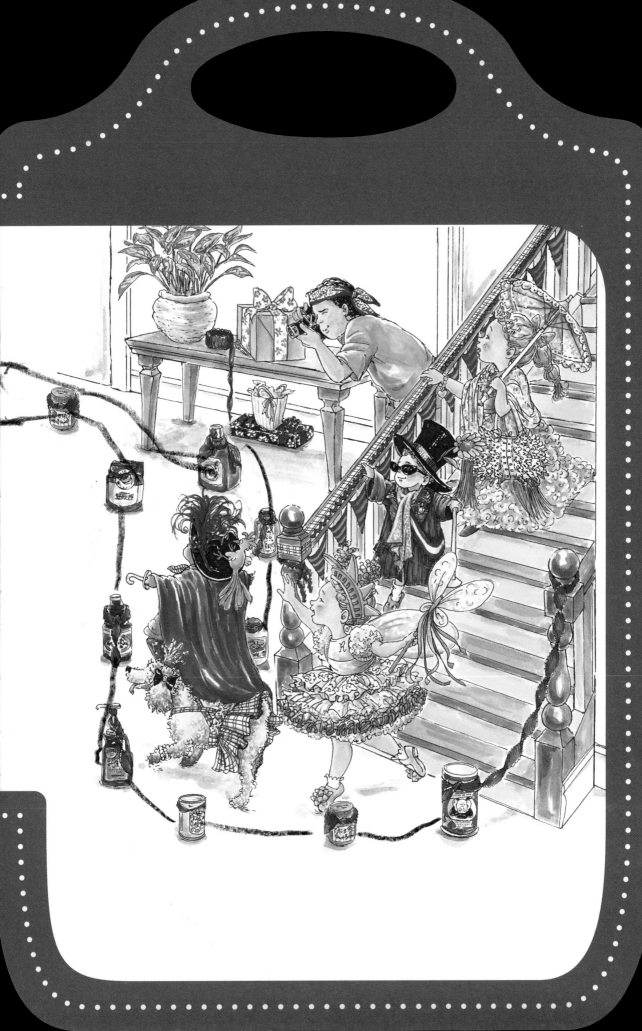

Go Bananas!

Nancy and her friends are practicing how to walk like models by balancing bananas on their heads. Place a banana sticker on each person's head.

Party On

No birthday party is complete without hats.
Color these party hats and decorate them with
your stickers so they look party-rrific.

A Walk in the Park

One of Nancy's favorite things is walking her dog, Frenchy (in style, of course!). Draw Nancy and a fancy leash for Frenchy.

Half Finished

Find the stickers to finish the picture.

Playtime with Frenchy

Frenchy has quite the collection of toys.
Can you color them in?

Frenchy: Fancy-Free

It's time to get ready for the dog pageant. Nancy hopes Frenchy will win first place. Help draw a tutu and tiara on her.

Nancy's mom's purse could use a little makeover. Draw shapes and designs on the purse to help transform it from bleak (drab) to chic (fab!).

Playdate

Bree is Nancy's best friend. Bree and Nancy are making best-friend necklaces for each other. Help color them in!

Perfect Pastries

Nancy is baking special cookies (with frosting!) for a class bake sale. Draw colorful decorations on the cookies!

A Perfect Picnic

A fabulous picnic requires an abundance (that means a lot) of treats. But some things on this page don't belong at a picnic. Circle what does not belong.

Fancy Stuff

Yummy Tummy Chocolate Sauce

Tea Sandwiches

Nancy loves tea sandwiches because they are so dainty. Each of these sandwiches is in the shape of a triangle, a square, or a circle. Draw a line to match each sandwich on the tray to its shape on the opposite page.

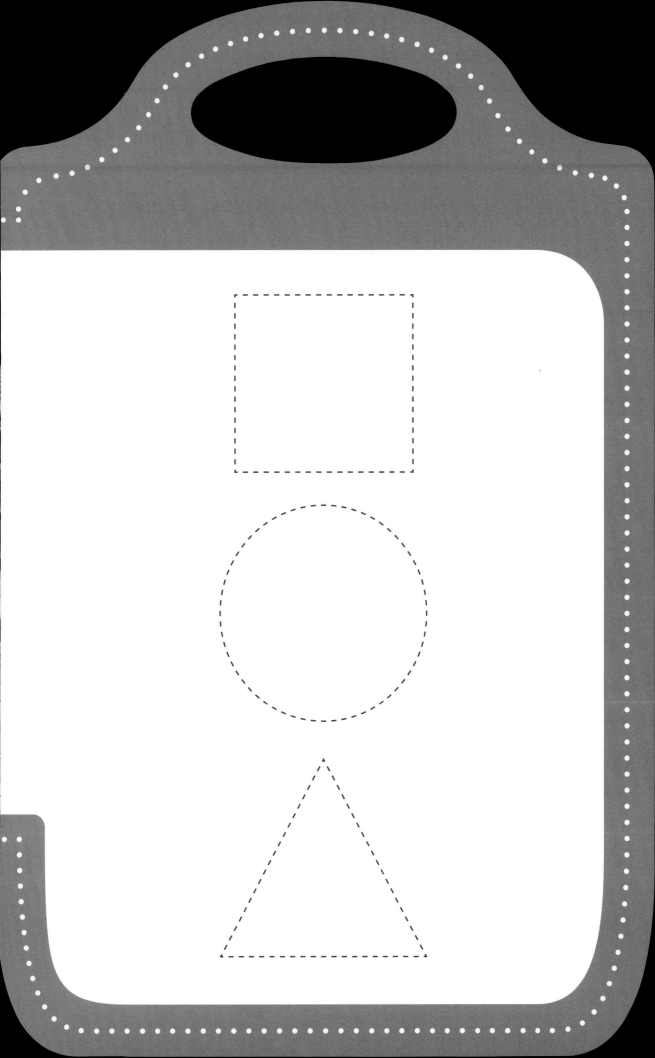

Silver-Screen Dreams

Nancy dreams of one day being a famous Hollywood star. Color in these movie-star accessories to turn these black-and-white Hollywood items into full color!

Ice Cream Social

The Clancy clan is headed to an old-fashioned soda
fountain (a fancy way of saying ice cream shop).
Color in this delicious ice cream sundae.
Add some cherries on top with your stickers.

Egg Hunt

Nancy is throwing an Easter egg hunt in her backyard.
Can you find and circle the 10 Easter eggs?

Butterfly Birthday

Butterfly birthday parties are Nancy's favorite.
Use your stickers to add butterflies, flowers, and hearts
(or draw your own) to this cake and color it in.

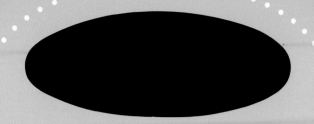

A Chic Chapeau

Nothing says fancy like a glamorous chapeau (that's French for hat). Color and decorate this hat with stickers to turn it from ordinary to extraordinary.

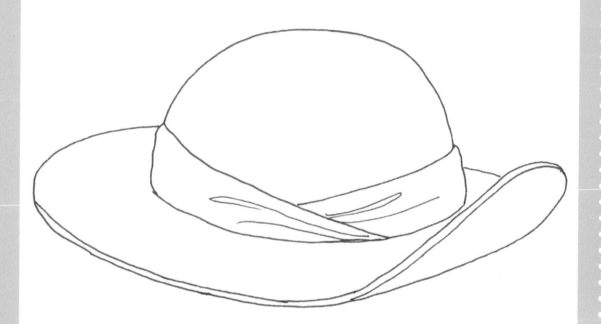

Oh no! These ladybugs are lost in Nancy's mom's garden.
Solve this maze to help get the ladybugs out of the garden.

Incredible Insects

How many bugs are on this spider web? Write the number of flies, ladybugs, and ants in the circles under each illustration.

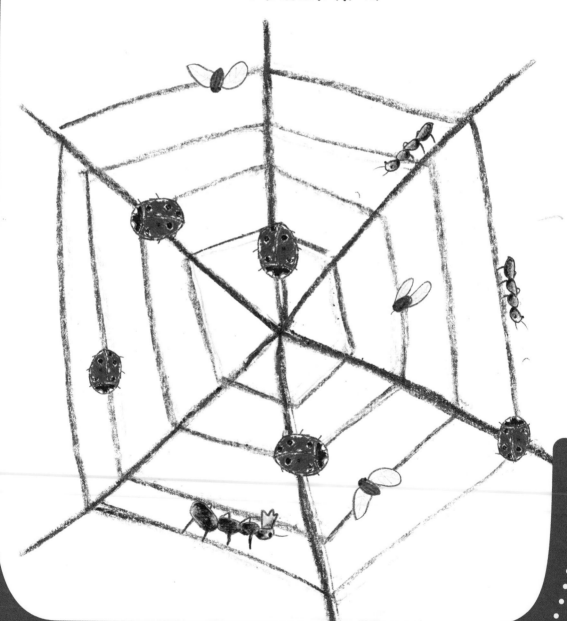

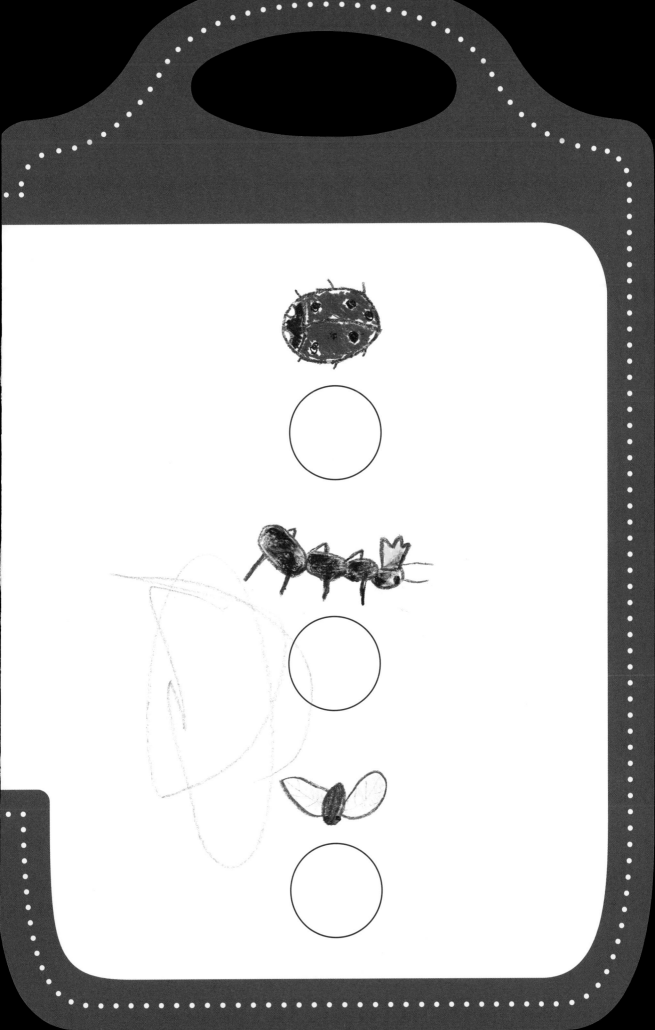

By the Fire

Find the stickers to finish the picture.

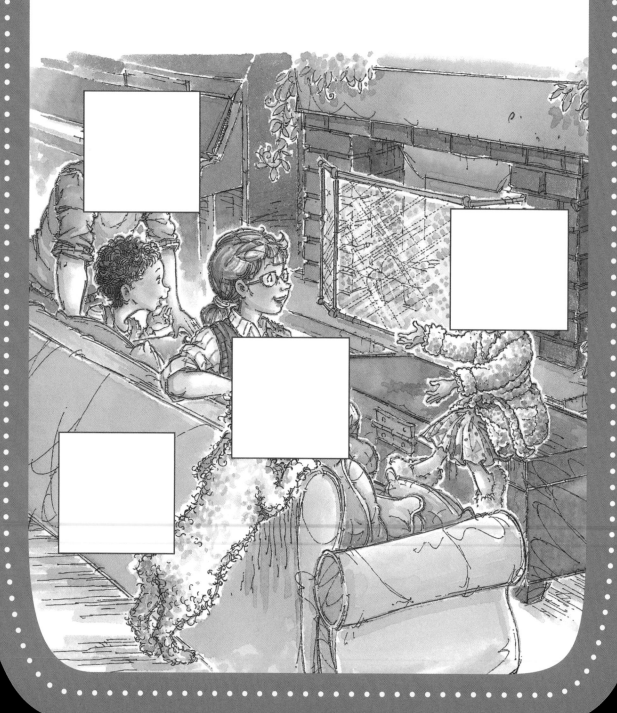

Seeing Stars

In school today, Ms. Glass taught everyone about constellations. A constellation is a group of stars that forms an image in the sky. Connect these stars to see which constellation is below.

Answer: Big Dipper

Frenchy Frolics

Frenchy loves to chase butterflies. Color in the butterflies and draw some more for Frenchy to frolic with.

Under the Sea

Find the stickers to finish the picture.

Nancy's Room

Nancy enjoys rotating (a fancy word for changing something often) the art she puts on her bedroom door. Help her by filling in the poster with something beautiful.

Express Yourself

Draw a self-portrait in this mirror.
Don't forget to strike a pose!

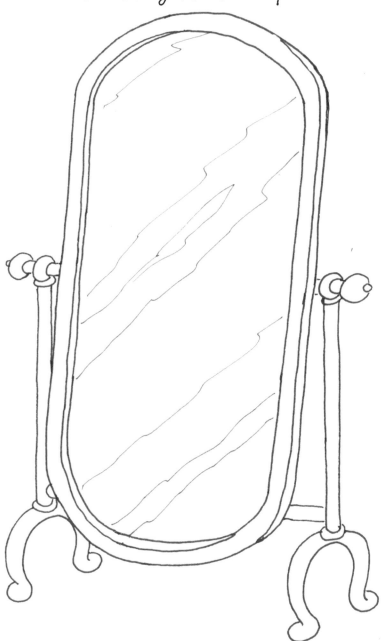

What's for Dinner?

Nancy's family is attending a very fancy soirée (a fancy word for party). What's being served for dinner? Draw it.

Crown Jewels

This crown needs some jewels to really make it regal (which is another word for magnificent). Decorate the crown with your jewel stickers.

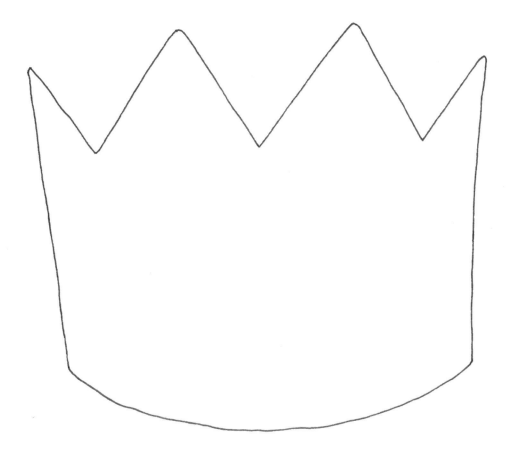

Heart to Heart

Nancy is making valentines for all her classmates.
Color in this heart.

Sleepy Time

Find the stickers to finish the picture.

Secret Admirer

Ooh la la! A valentine! Write your own message to someone special.

Arts and Crafts

Find the stickers to finish the picture.

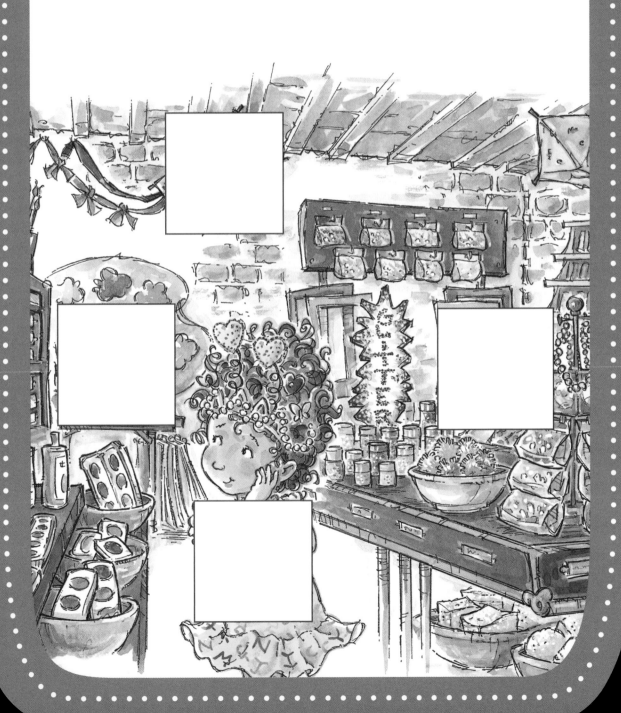

Pillow Fight

This is Nancy's bedroom. On the facing page, draw your bedroom.

Beauty Rest

Nancy's doll Marabelle would like to get some rest after a long day of tea parties. But she needs a bed! Finish the drawing of the bed to give Marabelle something comfy to lie on.

Make a Wish

This wand is almost fit for a magical princess. Color in the wand and decorate it with stickers.

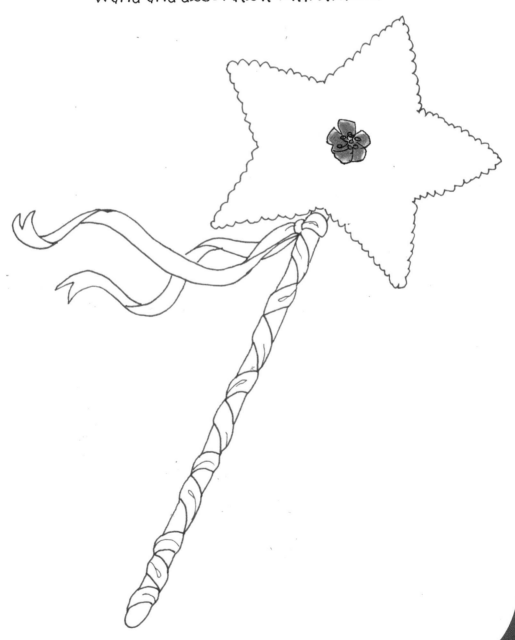

Swing Fling

This branch needs a swing.
Draw a swing and someone playing on it.

Life's a Beach

Nancy and her friends are building the ultimate sand castle. Before the waves wash it away, draw a door and some windows, and then decorate it.

Shoe-tastrophe

Oh no! These shoes are all mixed up! Match each one to its correct partner so that there are six matching pairs.

First Snowman

It's the first snow day of the year. Nancy made a snowman.
Help her decorate it.

Queen for a Day

Nancy loves anything royal. Today she is dressing up as a queen. Draw a crown on her head and one on Marabelle's.

Don't Judge a Book by Its Cover

Nancy adores reading. But what is she reading about? You decide, and then draw a cover for the book in her hands.

Practice Makes Perfect

Nancy likes to practice writing her name in different styles. Sometimes she writes her name in curlicues, and other times she writes it super-neat. Practice writing your own name.

Seeing Double

Two of JoJo's friends are twins. Sometimes JoJo wishes she had a twin. Draw another JoJo to make her dream come true.

Fancy Feet

Nancy wants to take these plain-looking shoes and make them gorgeous. Draw decorations on the shoes.

What's Old Is New Again

Nancy just bought something from her neighbor's garage sale. Draw something you just bought.

Show Us Your 'Stache

Nancy's sister, JoJo, is having a pirate-themed party.
Draw pirate mustaches on all the guests (Frenchy, too!).

For the Birds

Nancy is watching some birds up in a tree.
How many birds can you spot? Circle them.

Sensational Spa Cuisine

Mmmm. Nancy loves spa cuisine. She is making a healthy parfait, but some of the items are missing. Draw in your favorite ingredients.

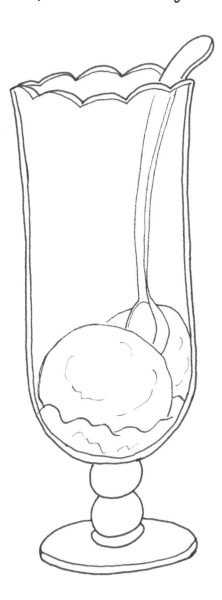

Dress-up Party

Find the stickers to finish the picture.

School Days

Decorate and color Nancy's first-day-of-school outfit.

Fairy Wings

Nancy and Bree are putting on a ballet all about fairies.
Draw fairy wings and color them a magical color.